Explorers

Searching for Adventure

Written by Gare Thompson

A Division of Harcourt Brace & Company

www.steck-vaughn.com

Contents

Explorers and Their Tools

Explorers travel to faraway places and return home to tell about their journeys. Some explorers start their new **adventures** on land. Some have underwater adventures. Explorers even go into outer space.

For thousands of years, people have wanted to learn about all of the different places on Earth. Some explored to find better places to live. Other explorers looked for food or drinking water. Some looked for treasure and adventure.

First, explorers found the seven **continents** on Earth. A globe shows the continents as large chunks of land. Great oceans and seas cover the rest of the Earth.

Over hundreds of years, people explored some continents by walking. Other continents could only be reached by ships. People explored the continents around the North Pole and the South Pole by using dog sleds across the snow and ice.

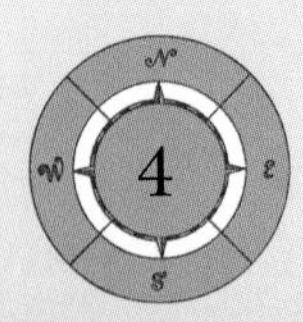

Many early explorers traveled by ship.

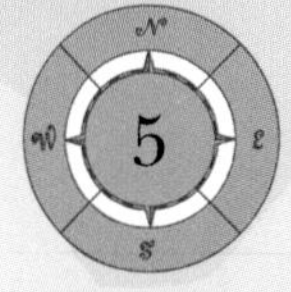

The first explorers traveled by land and by water. There were many tools to help them. Wheels made travel over land easier. Carts and wagons made it easier for people to carry food, clothes, and supplies. Rafts, boats, and sails let people travel over water.

Travelers used maps and charts to find good **routes** to places. They used a **compass** to help them go in the right direction. They also used the sun and the stars to find their way.

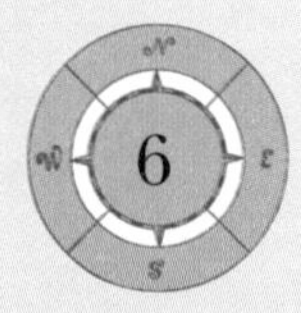

Tools like this astrolabe helped early explorers.

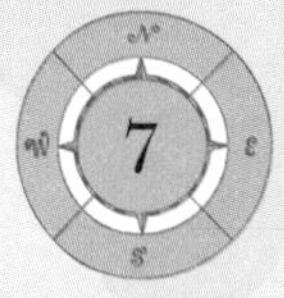

Early Explorers

The Vikings were people who lived in northern Europe about 1,000 years ago. They traveled over land and over water in search of new farmland. The Vikings were some of the first people to explore new places by ship.

One Viking explorer, Eric the Red, sailed to a new land that he named

Greenland. Later, his son, Leif Ericson, traveled even farther south to a land where grapes were growing. So he named that land Wineland. He left no maps, so no one is sure where that land was.

Leif Ericson and his crew traveled by sea.

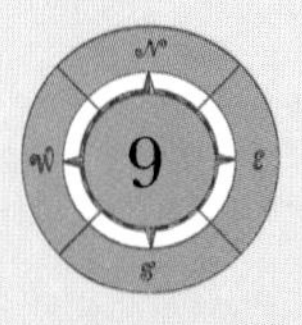

Many years later, two brothers from Italy went on a long trip to Asia. They were Maffeo and Nicolo Polo. The trip took nine years. Later Nicolo's son, Marco Polo, traveled with them to Asia. He was only 17 years old when he left home.

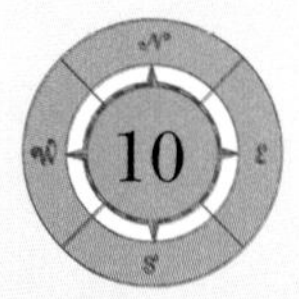

Marco Polo returned home from the big adventure 24 years later! He had traveled nearly 15,000 miles. He wrote a book about all his exciting adventures. The book made others want to explore new places, too.

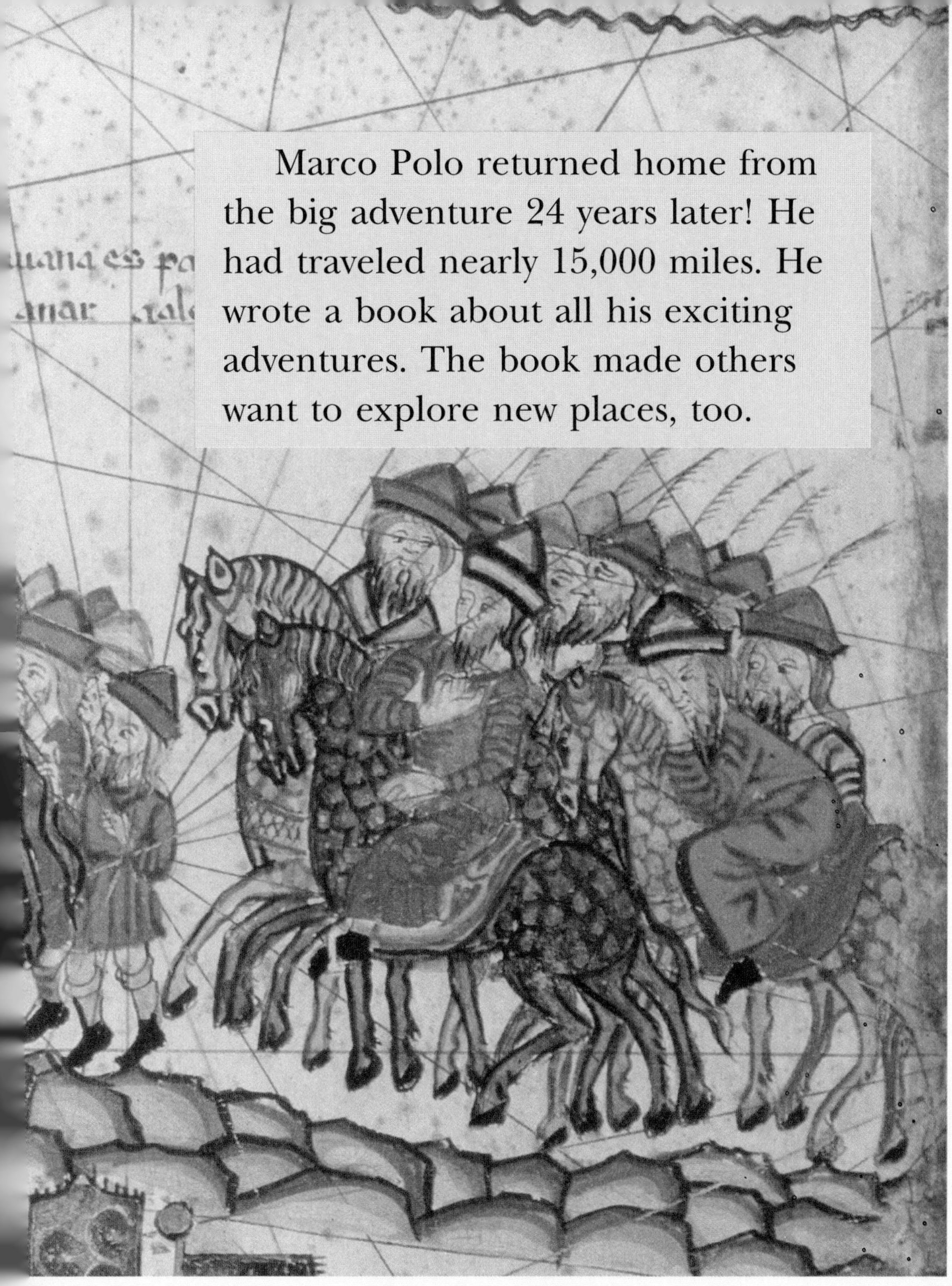

Marco Polo explored Asia.

About 200 years later, Prince Henry of Portugal did something to help explorers. He opened a school to teach sailors how to find their way on the open water. This study of finding good routes for travel is called **navigation**.

Prince Henry wanted sailors to explore the oceans. He paid for many of their **voyages**. After that time, most of the Earth could be explored and then mapped.

Sailors learned how to find their way in navigation school.

Around the World

Christopher Columbus was born in Italy in 1451. He went to sea as a very young man. His ship was wrecked once, so he became a mapmaker.

Columbus believed that the world was round, not flat. Not many people agreed with him. He believed that he

could travel to Asia by sailing across the Atlantic Ocean.

It took Columbus seven years to get enough money to pay for the trip. Finally, King Ferdinand and Queen Isabella of Spain helped him with ships and money. With three ships and a crew of 120 men, he set sail for Asia.

Columbus met with the King and Queen of Spain.

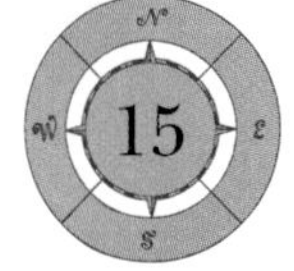

But the three ships landed on an island. Columbus was not in Asia. He had landed in a different place than he expected. He was in what is now called the Americas. Columbus later made three more voyages to the Americas, but he never reached Asia.

Many great explorers followed the route of Columbus. Stories of his trips led more people to explore North America and South America.

Christopher Columbus took three ships on his first voyage.

Magellan's crew sailed around the world.

After the travels of Christopher Columbus, Ferdinand Magellan also thought he could find a route to Asia by sea. In 1519, he set sail with five ships and 241 crew members. On the way, they had bad weather, illness, and shipwrecks. Magellan and many other men died on the trip.

After three long years, only one ship with eighteen men left on it got back home. They had proved that it was possible to sail all the way around the Earth. One man wrote down the events of the voyage, so many people learned more about sailing the oceans.

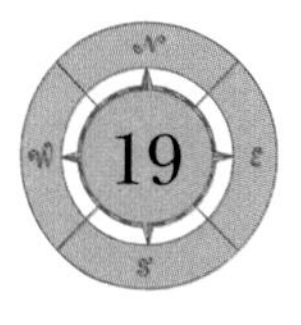

Exploring the Americas

As more people settled in the Americas, explorers drew maps and wrote about the mountains, deserts, and rivers. They wrote about plants and animals and the people they met on their voyages.

In the early 1800s, Meriwether Lewis and William Clark explored and mapped much of the United States. With the help of Sacagawea, a Native American, Lewis and Clark traveled up the Missouri River. They crossed over the Rocky Mountains, and went on west to the Pacific Ocean. Then they traveled all the way back east to Missouri. They had explored 6,000 miles of new land in two years!

Sacagawea guided Lewis and Clark.

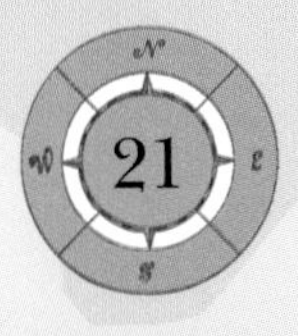

To the Poles

Up until the early 1900s, the North Pole and the South Pole had not been explored. Both are covered with ice and snow all year long. Robert Peary and Matthew Henson had tried many times to reach the North Pole. Peary sailed a ship that moved through ice. They traveled over ice fields on land with dog sleds. They finally reached the North Pole in 1909.

Later, two groups of explorers raced to reach the South Pole. Roald Amundsen's great skill with dog sleds helped his group get to the South Pole five weeks before another group arrived in 1911.

Robert Peary explored the North Pole.

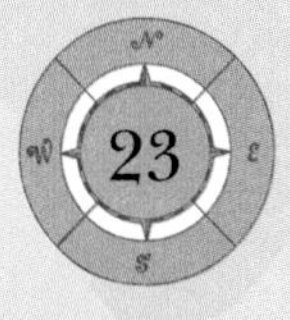

Deep Seas and High Mountains

The life under the seas had not yet been explored. Jacques Cousteau was one of the first to explore life under the sea. He invented some special tools to help explore the oceans. He helped invent gear for divers so they could breathe underwater.

Beginning in 1951, Cousteau led a special **research** ship. The crew of this ship made maps of the ocean floor and studied sea life. They measured water flow and temperature. They also searched for oil and minerals. Cousteau wrote books and made films about sea life.

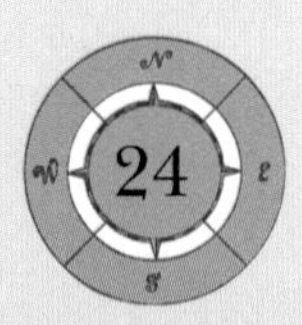

Divers use special gear to explore underwater.

Not only did people explore the deepest seas, but they also explored the highest mountains. The highest mountain on Earth is Mount Everest.

Many mountain climbers had tried to climb this steep mountain that has high winds and thin air. Then in 1953, Sir Edmund Hillary and his guide, Tenzing Norgay, reached the top. It was a brave adventure.

Since then, other climbers have reached the top of Mount Everest and have studied many mountains.

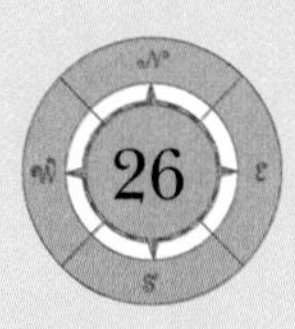

Hillary and Norgay first reached the top of Mount Everest.

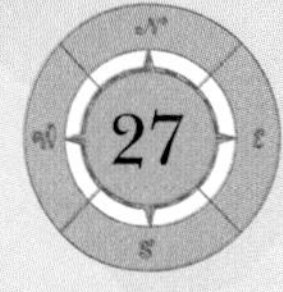

Into Space

Explorers have studied many places on Earth, and some explorers have even been to outer space. In 1961, a Russian pilot named Yuri Gagarin was the first to travel in space to **orbit** the Earth.

In 1970, Neil Armstrong and Edwin Aldrin were the first people to walk on the moon. In 1996, Dr. Shannon Lucid spent 188 days studying the Earth aboard a Russian space station. That is a long time to be away from the Earth!

Edwin Aldrin walked on the moon.

Dr. Shannon Lucid trained for her trip into space.

What other places do you think can be explored? New explorers might learn more about mountains, caves, deserts, oceans, and outer space. They might learn more about rocks from the moon or from Venus or Mars. Who knows what is going to be discovered next? Maybe you will be the next explorer to find out.

There are many places to explore beyond Earth.

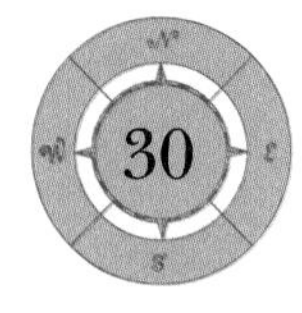

Glossary

adventures things a person does that are exciting and dangerous

compass tool that shows North, East, South, and West

continents the seven main land areas on Earth

explorers people who travel to new places to find what is there

navigation planning and guiding good routes for travel

orbit the path a spacecraft takes as it moves around the Earth

research studying things to find out more

routes ways to go

voyages trips